A FLOCK OF FUN

BY Raven Howell
Illustrated by David Barrow

Doodle and Peck Publishing
P.O. Box 852105
Yukon, Oklahoma 73085

(405) 354-7422

doodleandpeck.com

Howell, Raven
A Flock of Fun/ by Raven Howell; illustrated by David Barrow
Summary: When the moon shines brightly, a young child decides to count sheep to go to sleep. He discovers the sheep are too mischievous so he decides to count snails. After a night with the quiet, slow, slimy snails, he finds that maybe the sheep and their antics will be better to count after all.

ISBN 978-1-7337170-8-3 (hard)   ISBN 978-1-7333462-2-1 (soft)
1. Sleep—Fiction 2. Sheep—Fiction 3. Snails—Fiction 4. Moon—Fiction 5. Illustrator--David Barrow

[E]

Library of Congress Number 2019946372

Dedication

To you, the reader—may you enjoy countless warm and fluffy dreams!

Raven Howell

For Randy who gives me so many fun things to ponder that keep me up at night.

David Barrow

Moonlight shone so bold and bright,

it kept me wide awake at night.

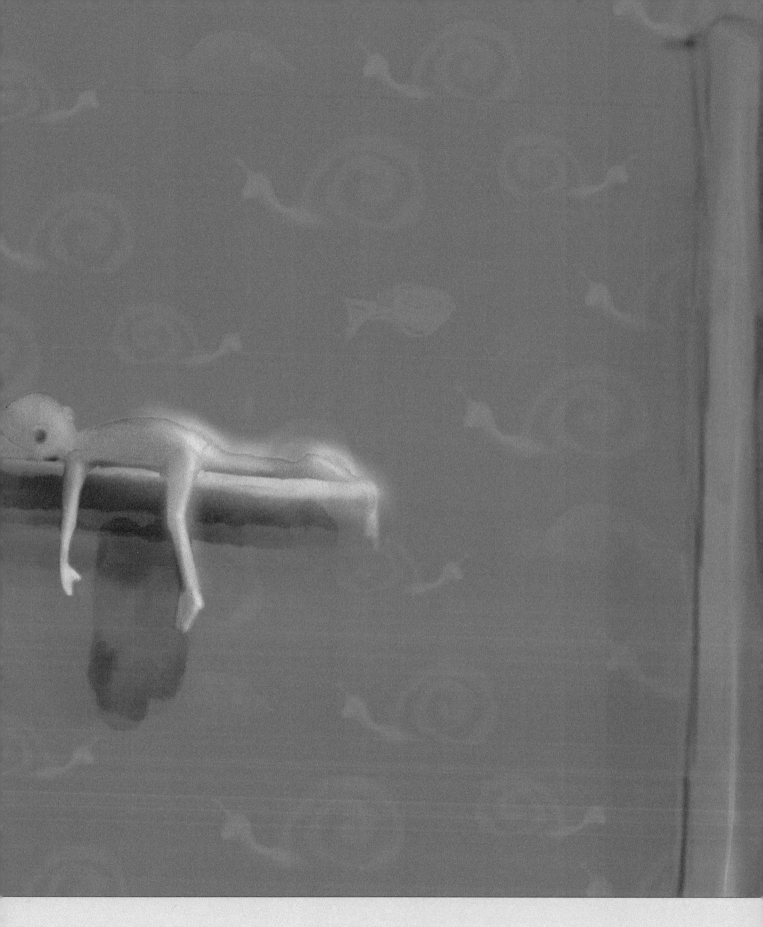

To try to sleep

I counted sheep.

But they're a noisy flock of bleat,
with no polite, no nice, no neat.

Not one would stop and take a seat.

**Apparently, happy to meet
me in my bed, under the sheet,**

where fluffy lambs tickled my feet
and mocked, with "Meow" and "Moo!" and "Cheep!"

They dumped my toy chest, swung from my lamp,
played games wearing my underpants!

Sheep laundry-dived and scribbled pictures,
swirled shirts in neon tie-dye mixtures.

They read my books out loud for fun—
"Sheep in a Jeep," their favorite one.

They ate my candy stash and chips,
then asked for cheese and spinach dips.

Eventually, my eyes did sag.
The sheep themselves began to lag.

They snugged on shelves, they tucked in drawers,
hammocked curtains, sprawled on floors.

Tired now, I dozed in bed

and thought, "I *should* count snails instead!"

The next night came.

So did the snails,

leaving silver glistening trails.

**At first, I didn't mind, but then
I grew impatient, wondered when**

we'd paint our pictures, sing our songs.
It felt as if something was wrong!

Until the snails began to snore

sleeping seemed to be a chore.

Then I knew I'd rather keep

my noisy laundry-diving sheep!

Raven Howell is an award-winning children's author and poet of nine picture books. She writes poetry for a variety of children's magazines including Highlights, The School Magazine, Humpty Dumpty, and Cricket. Frequently sharing book presentations and writing workshops with children in schools and libraries, Raven also serves as Creative & Publishing Advisor with Red Clover Reader.

Raven Howell, Author

David Barrow spent his happiest hours in the school library. It was there he read books about famous people and learned how to draw. After working as a graphic designer, camera man, and video editor, Barrow embarked on his lifelong dream of illustrating children's books. David has illustrated nine books for Doodle and Peck Publishing.

David Barrow, Illustrator

Doodle and Peck Publishing produces fun, family-friendly books, created by talented authors and illustrators. Most of our books have a curriculum connection, making them not just entertaining, but educational. Many of our authors and illustrators visit schools and libraries sharing their passion for great literature.

Our company uses recycled materials for much of our shipping. And last, but not least, Doodle and Peck books are printed right here in the USA.

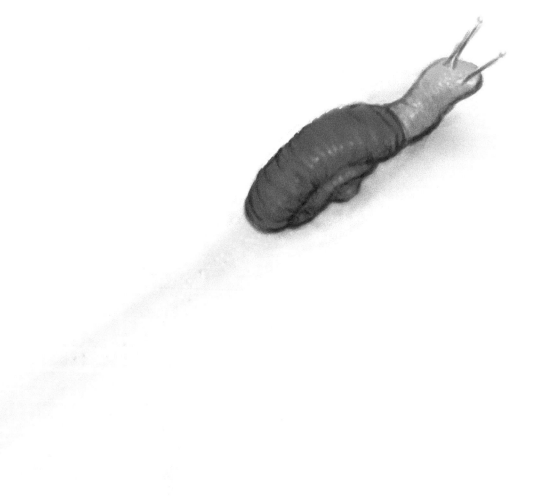

www.doodleandpeck.com

CPSIA information can be obtained
at www.ICGtesting.com
Printed in the USA
BVHW020200250320
575914BV00002B/8